The Meat Eaters Arrive

Suzan Reid ❋ Linda Hendry

FIREFLY BOOKS

For Grandma Harder.
L.H.

To Nicol and Devyn.
S.R.

A FIREFLY BOOK

Published in the U.S. in 1996 by:
Firefly Books (U.S.) Inc.
P.O. Box 1338
Ellicott Station
Buffalo, New York 14207

6 5 4 3 2 1   Printed in Canada   6 7 8 9/9

Cataloguing in Publication Data

Reid, Suzan, 1963-
  The meat eaters arrive

ISBN 1-55209-004-3

1. Picture books for children. I. Hendry, Linda.
II. Title.

PS8585. E607M4 1996   jC813'.54   C95-932459-3
PZ7.R45Me 1996

The Brontos lived in a very quiet neighbourhood.
Everyone moved around slowly, planting shrubs and
trees, eating shrubs and trees, and hanging laundry on
very long clotheslines.

They would chat about the change in weather, and on warmer days the Brontos would invite their neighbours over for a pool party.

The Iggys and the Steggys and the Ceratops
would wander over and slip into the very large pool,
and they always had lots of fun.

Right beside the Brontos' was a very large house
for sale. Everyone wondered who would move in.
"I hope they like to swim," Mrs. Bronto said.

"I hope they plant ferns," Mr. Bronto said.
"I hope they like computer games," all the little
Brontos said. So they all hoped and waited together.

555 - 79231

One day, a very large moving van pulled up with a screech in front of the empty house. The neighbours watched from their windows as furniture was unloaded. Then the car came. It was a very large black

convertible. Out stepped Mr. and Mrs. Rex and five little Rexes. The neighbours gasped. The neighbours closed their curtains. Then the neighbours locked their doors and ran into their basements.

"How long do we have to stay down here?" a little Bronto asked.

"Until they move, dear," answered Mrs. Bronto from behind a very large chair.

"Everybody be quiet," Mr. Bronto whispered from inside a closet.

So everyone was quiet. Very quiet. They stayed in the basement for days. Everyone was getting hungry, and Brontos make very loud gurgling noises when they are hungry.

"We're too noisy," Mr. Bronto whispered from his closet.

"I'll go get some ferns," volunteered Mrs. Bronto, and away she went in search of food.

When Mrs. Bronto got to the top of the stairs, she noticed a shiny white envelope on the floor by the front door. She grabbed it. It read:

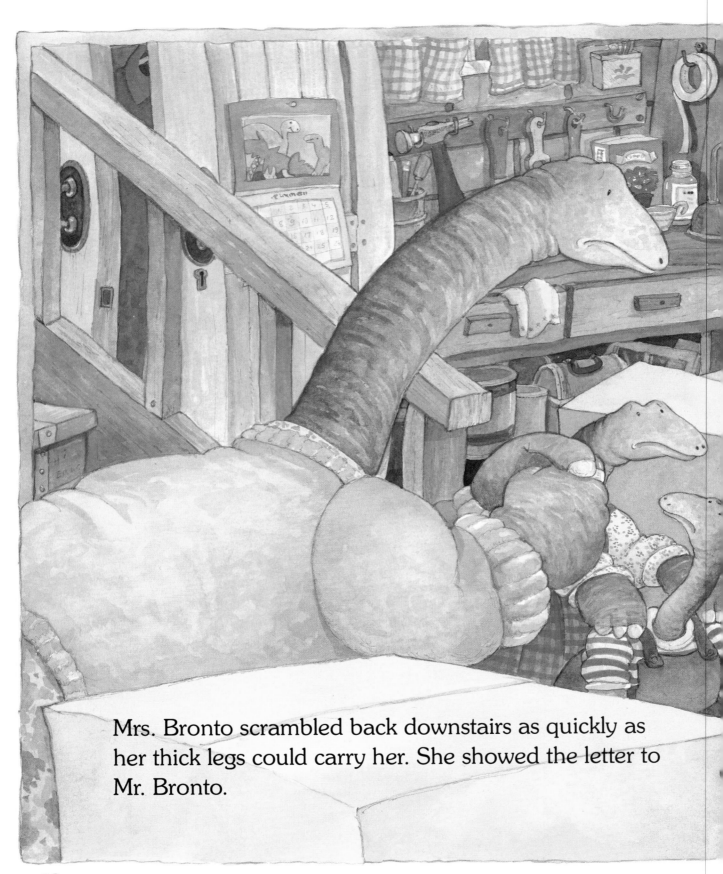

Mrs. Bronto scrambled back downstairs as quickly as her thick legs could carry her. She showed the letter to Mr. Bronto.

"I've heard of unfriendly, but this really makes me mad. Imagine! Inviting us . . . to be eaten!" he huffed, and he shuffled back into his closet.

Saturday came. The Brontos shook with fear.

Late that afternoon, Mr. Bronto climbed out of his closet and sniffed the air. There was a strange smell.

"What's that?" he asked.

"I've never smelled anything like that before," Mrs. Bronto said as she stepped out from behind her chair. Together they crept out of the basement, following the smell. It carried them out the patio doors and into the backyard. Very quietly, they peered over the back fence . . .

Mr. Rex was standing on his patio
wearing an apron that said "Kiss the Cook."
He looked up and smiled. His teeth sparkled.
His eyes danced. There was drool coming out of his
very large mouth.

"You're here!" he shouted. "Well, come on over!
Hey, we thought nobody would show. We've got steaks
on the sizzle for us, and Mrs. Rex is inside chopping up
some greens for you vegetarian folk. Man, is this
neighbourhood dead or what? Haven't seen a soul for a
week. Come on, let's get some grub happening here!"

17

Mr. and Mrs. Bronto looked at each other. Mrs. Rex brought out the Caesar salad. Mr. Rex flipped a steak. They had a great time. They ate and ate. The kids played computer games. They planted some new shrubs.

And they sat by the pool, chatting about the change in weather, until the sun went down.

21

The End